# all that
# I Am

Written by M.H. Clark
Illustrated by Laura Carlin

When the night sky is high like a ceiling of stars,
I look up at the face of the moon.
*What do you see*, I ask, *there where you are?*
And the moon says, *right now, I see you.*

I count the bright hundreds of waves on the sea
as they crash and they rush to the shore.
And I let those waves touch their cold hands to my feet.
*Roar*, say the waves, so I roar.

And I look at the flowers that grow in the field
as they turn their heads up to the sky.
So I turn my head too, just to feel what they feel
with the sun and the wind blowing by.

I am bright like you, moon, and I shine in my way,
I am loud as the waves on the sand,
I can move like the flowers move every day,
but this still isn't all that I am.

The tops of the evergreens speak with the clouds
while their roots dig down steady and deep.
I can reach the sky too, so I lift my head proud,
with the earth below holding my feet.

All the raindrops are whispering *hush* as they fall,
and they land on the earth with a kiss.
I can touch the world too, even though I am small.
Like the rain, what I am is a gift.

Then the storm, with its flashes of light, passes through
and it opens the sky with a crack.
I am big just like that, and I'm powerful too.
So I clap when the thunderbolts clap.

I am strong as the trees that stand ancient and wise,
I'm giving and soft as the rain.
I am brilliant and huge as a blaze in the skies,
but that still isn't all that I am.

The wide river sparkles and rushes along
through the rocks and the hills to the sea.
I follow and sing an adventuring song.
We are brave, the wide river and me.

The mountain lifts up its strong shoulders of stone,
and it stands for a very long time.
I am strong like that too, in a way all my own,
and my body's a mountain that's mine.

When the sun paints the sky pink and orange and blue,
with its light that is brilliant and clear,
I say, *I want to make the world beautiful too,*
and the sun says, *that's why you are here.*

I am bold as the river that makes its own way,
I am huge as the high mountain peaks.
Like the sun, I bring color and light to the day,
but there's still more than that inside me.

There are wonders inside me that no one yet knows,
there is magic the world's never seen.
There are seeds for a future that grows as I grow,
there are so many things I will be.

And the sun and the stars and the trees and the land,
and the rain and the storm and the sea
love me here in this moment for all that I am—
and for all of the worlds within me.

*Written by:* M.H. Clark

*Illustrated by:* Laura Carlin

*Edited by:* Amelia Riedler

*Art Directed by:* Heidi Dyer and Megan Gandt Guansing

Library of Congress Control Number: 2020944701 | ISBN: 978-1-970147-46-9

1st printing. Printed in China with soy inks on FSC®-Mix certified paper. A012103001

*Create meaningful moments with gifts that inspire.*

CONNECT WITH US

live-inspired.com  |  sayhello@compendiuminc.com

    @compendiumliveinspired
#compendiumliveinspired